WHO'S LOOKING AT YOU?

Can you identify these animals by looking into their eyes?

chimpanzee
fish
frog
owl
parrot
tiger

1.

2.

3.

4.

5.

6.

J. HUNT

TRICK OR TREASURE?

You have found this painting on one of the Great Pyramids in Egypt. Have you discovered an ancient treasure? How do you know?

THE HAIRCUT

Professor Crumbell spent a year in the jungle studying lions. When he returned home, he *looked* like a lion! His hairdresser helped him. Number the pictures to show what happened first, second, and so on.

Illustrated by John Nez

Answer on page 47.

NUTS AND BOLTS

This code is as hard as nails. Each type of fastener stands for one of two letters.

For example  sometimes stands for A and other times for N. Can you hammer out the names of eight things you might find at a hardware store?

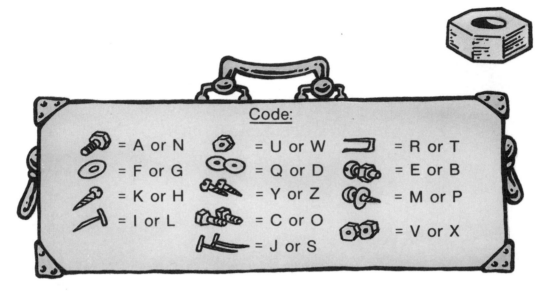

Code:

= A or N   = U or W   = R or T
= F or G   = Q or D   = E or B
= K or H   = Y or Z   = M or P
= I or L   = C or O   = V or X
     = J or S

1. __ __ __ __ __ __

2. __ __ __ __ __

3. __ __ __ __ __ __ __ __ __ __

4. __ __ __ __

5. __ __ __ __ __ __ __

6. __ __ __ __ __ __ __ __ __ __

7. __ __ __ __ __ __ __ __ __ __

Illustrated by Jerry Zimmerman

COOL IT

Your tired dad has just returned from the store with two big bags of groceries. As you help him put things away, which ones will you put into the refrigerator?

Answer on page 47.

MISSING LETTER

Which letter is missing from the scrambled alphabet below?

Answer on page 47.

SCRAMBLED BIRDS

Why do hummingbirds hum? To find out, unscramble the birds, *a* through *m*. Then move the numbered letters to the answer spaces.

a. VODE <u>D</u> <u>O</u> <u>V</u> <u>E</u>
      12

b. WORC __ __ __ __
            8

c. WHAK __ __ __ __
           5

d. SNAW __ __ __ __
     9

e. BRION __ __ __ __ __
     2

f. KROST __ __ __ __ __
        11

g. OSEGO __ __ __ __ __
     7

h. GOPINE __ __ __ __ __ __
          10

i. TRORAP __ __ __ __ __ __
            4

j. WRAPROS __ __ __ __ __ __ __
    13

k. UPENING __ __ __ __ __ __ __
       3

l. GLOMIFAN __ __ __ __ __ __ __ __
          6

m. INDRACLA __ __ __ __ __ __ __ __
      1

Answer:

Because they __ __ __ __ , __ __ __ __
        1 2 3 4   5 6 7 8

the __ __ __ <u>D</u> __ .
    9 10 11 12 13

Illustrated by Holly Kowitt

Answer on page 47.

DOWN-ON-THE-FARM CROSSWORD

Welcome to the farm! These pictures will tell you what words
to write in the spaces across and down.

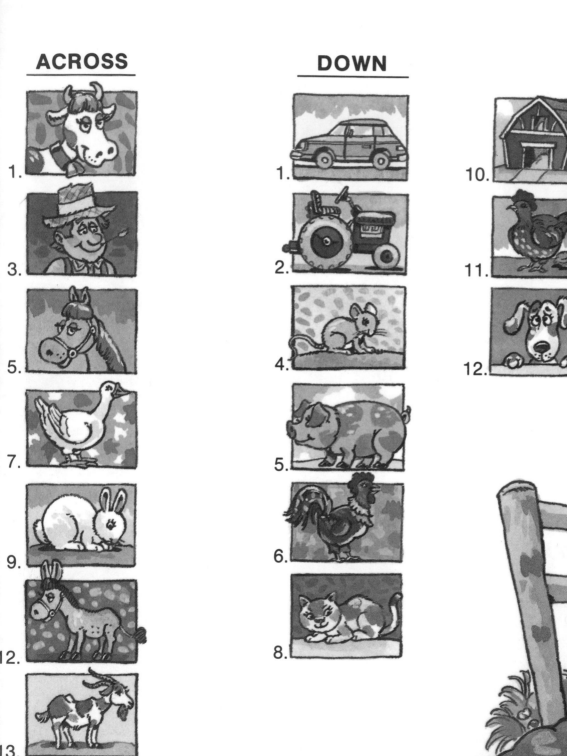

ACROSS

1.

3.

5.

7.

9.

12.

13.

DOWN

1.

2.

4.

5.

6.

8.

10.

11.

12.

Answer on page 47.

CLIMB TIME

Help this mountain climber make it to the top.

Answer on page 48.

Illustrated by Pat Merrell

DOT'S DEPARTMENT STORE

When the Martin family went camping in the mountains they forgot to pack some very important items. In the nearest town they shopped at Dot's to buy the things they needed. Connect the dots of the same color to find out what camping equipment they had to purchase.

Answer on page 48.

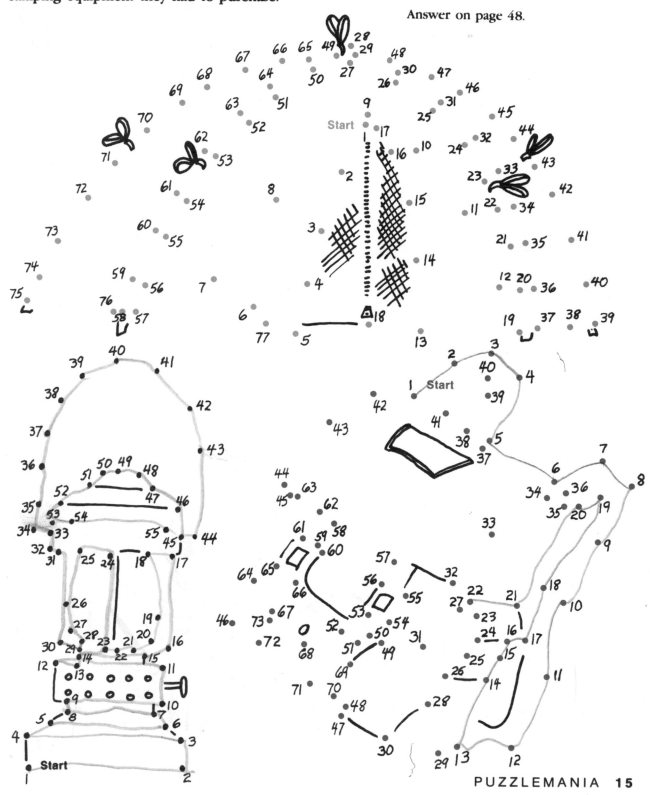

EYE FOOLERS

Look at the pictures and answer the questions.
Be careful. Your eyes can fool you!

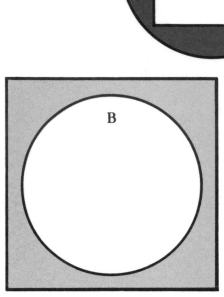

1. Which person is the tallest?

2. Which circle is bigger?

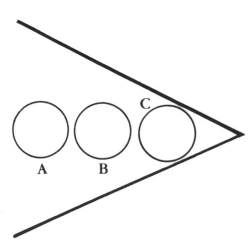

3. Which circle is largest?

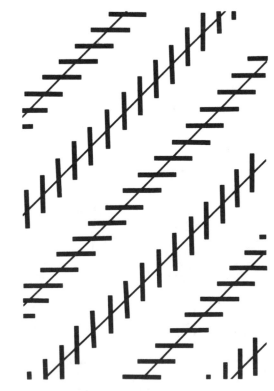

4. Are the thin lines parallel / / / or not / \ / ?

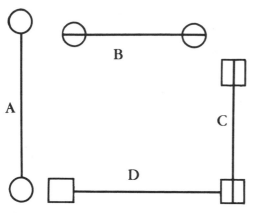

A

B

C

D

5. Which line is the longest?

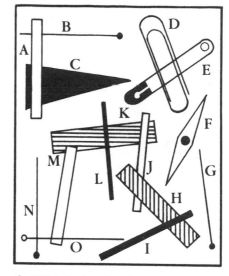

6. Which is the longest object?

7. Which thin line is longer?

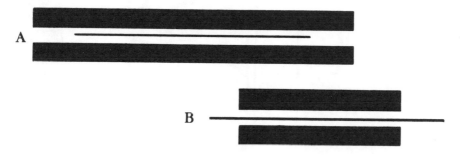

A

B

8. Which moon is larger?

CHECKER CHECK

How many things can you find wrong in this picture?

WOOD SEARCH

Eleven kinds of trees are hidden in the "forest" of letters below. See if you can find them. Look up, down, sideways, backward, and diagonally.

ASH   ELM   PALM

OAK   APPLE   CHERRY

CEDAR MAPLE PECAN

PEAR   FIG

C	H	E	R	R	Y
F	E	L	P	P	A
I	L	D	E	E	P
G	P	C	A	A	H
O	A	K	L	R	S
N	M	M	L	E	A

Illustrated by Paul Richer

Answer on page 48.

DIGBY'S DINNER

Digby the dog forgot where he buried his bone. To find it, use the clues below. You will need a ruler.

1. Start at the tree that is exactly one inch tall.

2. Go from that tree to the nearest house.

3. Count the number of windows. Starting at the front door, go directly west that number of inches. Then turn and go south.

4. If you come to a tree first, turn and go west. If you come to a rock first, turn and go east.

5. When you reach a house, turn and go north five inches. Go to the nearest house. Then go west three and a half inches.

Congratulations!
You've found where Digby's bone is buried.
Where is it?

Answer on page 48.

TAKE IT TO THE TOP

Help Homer find his way to the roof so he can deliver a very important message.

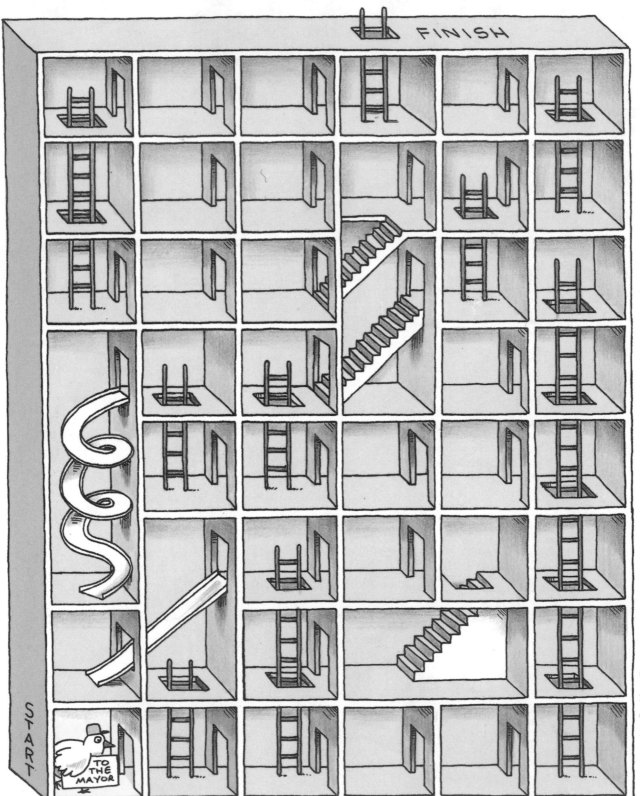

Answer on page 48.

WHAT ON EARTH?

To answer the worldly question below, find each letter by moving the number of spaces in the direction given. Place each letter in its numbered space. Always begin at the *. The first letter has been found for you.

Worldly Question:
When do you become a South American country?

1. North-1
2. South-1
3. East-2
4. West-1
5. Northeast-1
6. Southwest-1
7. Southeast-2
8. Northwest-2

9. Northeast-2
10. South-1, Southwest-1
11. North-1, Northeast-1
12. West-2
13. North-1, Northwest-1
14. East-1, Northeast-1
15. South-1, Southeast-1

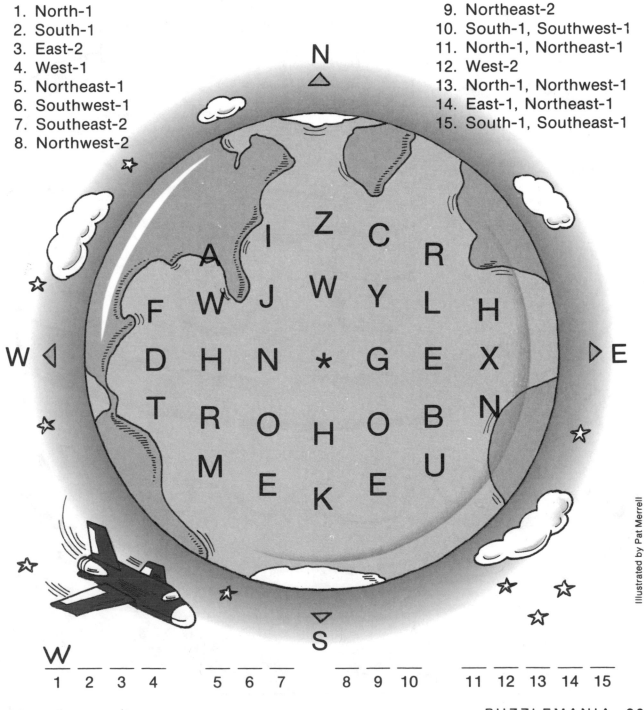

W __ __ __ __   __ __ __   __ __ __   __ __ __ __ __
  1 2 3 4   5 6 7   8 9 10   11 12 13 14 15

Answer on page 49.

Illustrated by Pat Merrell

PIECE OF CAKE

Which two pieces on the right did not come from this cake?

Illustrated by Jerry Zimmerman

Answer on page 49.

A.

B.

C.

D.

E.

F.

G.

H.

DOZENS OF Ds

There are at least twenty-four things in this picture that begin with the letter D. How many can you find?

Answer on page 49.

CARRY ON

What are these people carrying? Use your imagination and draw your answer.

Illustrated by Barbara Gray

WHAT GOES WITH WHAT?

Each item on the left-hand page goes with something on the right-hand page. Can you match the things that belong together?

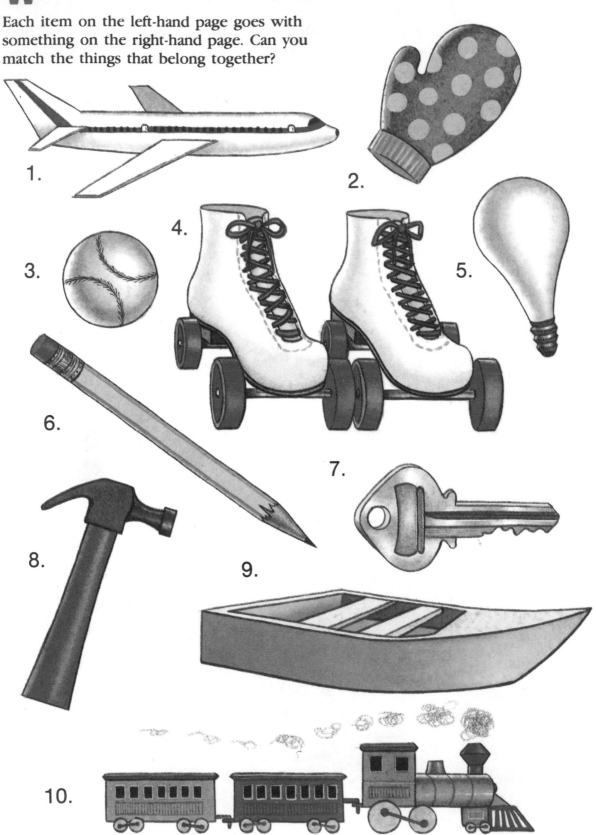

1.

2.

3.

4.

5.

6.

7.

8.

9.

10.

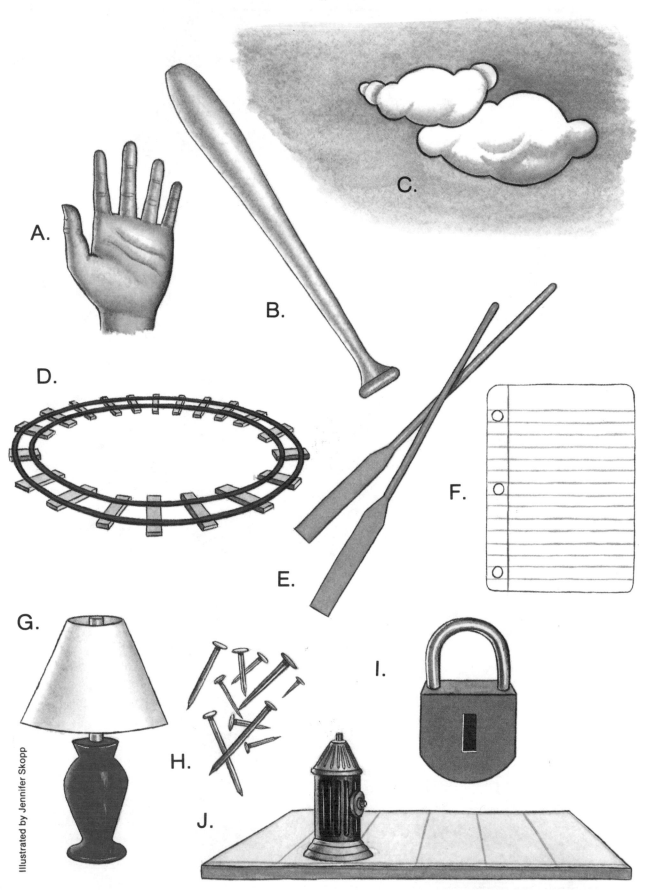

A.

B.

C.

D.

E.

F.

G.

H.

I.

J.

Answer on page 49.

HIDDEN PICTURES

There are at least 18 objects hidden in this picture. How many can you find?

TUMBLEWORDS

There are six scrambled words in this box. Every word has its own kind of letters. Find each group of letters, then unscramble them to find the sporty words.

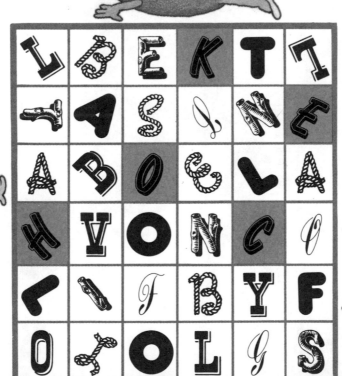

Answer on page 49.

Illustrated by Barbara Gray

INSTANT PICTURE

What's hidden on this page? To find out, fill
in every section that contains two dots.

Illustrated by McKenzie/Perrin

STOP, LOOK, AND LIST

Under each category, list one thing that begins with each letter. For example, one American city that begins with C is Cleveland. See if you can name another.

American Cities

T _____

C _____

P _____

B _____

O _____

Flowers

T _____

C _____

P _____

B _____

O _____

Breakfast Foods

T _____

C _____

P _____

B _____

O _____

Answer on page 49.

Illustrated by Doug Taylor

Seashore Memories
Part 1

Take a long look at this picture. Try to remember everything you see in it. Then turn the page, and try to answer some questions about it without looking back.

Illustrated by Barbara Gray

DON'T READ THIS UNTIL YOU HAVE LOOKED AT "Seashore—Part 1" Memories ON PAGE 35.

SEASHORE MEMORIES

Part 2

Can you answer these questions about the seaside scene you saw?

1. What did the boys make out of sand?
2. How many dolphins did you see?
3. What was one girl eating for a snack?
4. What color was the inner tube?
5. How many sailboats did you see?
6. Did anyone have a radio?
7. Who was sleeping?
8. How many people wore sunglasses?

Answer on page 49.

WHICH CLASSROOM?

Nathan, Sarah, and Ben wonder which classrooms they have for fifth grade. The teachers are Ms. Heinz, Mr. Franklin, and Ms. DeCaro. Use these clues to find the answers.

1. Ms. DeCaro will teach a child whose name ends in *n*.

2. Ben doesn't have a man for a teacher.

3. Sarah doesn't have the teacher with the longest name.

Basso

Answer on page 49

TEST PATTERNS

Which screen shows the most shapes?

1.

2.

3.

4.

Illustrated by Doug Taylor

Answer on page 49.

DINNER IS SERVED

Please help seat the guests at this special dinner party. Here are the guest list and a chart of the dining table. Who belongs in which seat?

Guest List
Humpty Dumpty
Miss Muffet and Guest
Mama Bear
Papa Bear
Baby Bear
Caterpillar
Curlylocks
Little Jack Horner
Old King Cole

tuffet web

large chair

medium chair

small chair

wall

mushroom

throne cushion corner

Answer on page 49.

OLD MEXICO

Here are some words that might make you think of old Mexico. Can you find them in the letters below? Look up, down, and sideways. Be careful. Some words overlap and some are written backwards.

SOMBRERO
PEPPER
TAMALES
POTTERY
PESO
RESORT
RANCH
LEMON
SOUTH
SIESTA
CACTUS
FUN
FIESTA
MULE
TACO
MUSIC
MESA
CLAY
SUN
CORN

```
S O M B R E R O A T Q
I N U F E B A L I Z P
E K S V S U N W I X E
S C I Z O E C L A Y S
T A C O R N H M T R O
A C M U T S D E S E M
D T A M A L E S E T B
M U L E M O N A I T R
C S O U T H A R F O M
F L G W R E P P E P G
```

Illustrated by John Nez

Answer on page 49.

SPEAKING IN COLOR

1. If your aunt says you have a GREEN THUMB it means . . .

   A. you are lucky.
   B. you can grow plants very well.
   C. you need money.

2. If your sister says she is SEEING RED it means . . .

   A. she is wearing sunglasses.
   B. she is visiting an eye doctor.
   C. she is angry.

3. If the hero of a story has a YELLOW STREAK it means . . .

   A. he colors his hair.
   B. he is an artist.
   C. he is not very brave.

4. If your neighbor is FEELING BLUE it means . . .

   A. she is frightened.
   B. she is very serious.
   C. she is sad.

Illustrated by Jerry Zimmerman

5. If you are WEARING ROSE-COLORED GLASSES it means . . .

   A. you are watching a 3-D movie.
   B. you have a lot of energy.
   C. you have a positive attitude.

6. If your friend says he is GREEN WITH ENVY it means . . .

   A. he is out of breath.
   B. he is jealous.
   C. he is seasick.

7. If your doctor says you're IN THE PINK it means . . .

   A. you are very warm.
   B. you are very healthy.
   C. you should get more exercise.

8. If your teacher says today is a RED-LETTER DAY it means . .

   A. report cards will be sent home.
   B. this is a very important day.
   C. today is Saturday.

Answer on page 50.

CRISSCROSS COUNTDOWN

Can you fit these words into the spaces at the right? The lists tell
how many letters are in each word. This will help you see where
they fit into the puzzle. It may help to cross each word off the list
when you put it in the puzzle.

Answer on page 50

Four Letters

CREW
FUEL
MOON

Ten Letters

ATMOSPHERE
SPACECRAFT

Eight Letters

ASTEROID
BLAST OFF

Nine Letters

ASTRONAUT
DISCOVERY
SATELLITE

Seven Letters

GRAVITY
MERCURY
SHUTTLE

Six Letters

APOLLO   OXYGEN
GEMINI   PLANET
LAUNCH   ROCKET
METEOR

Five Letters

COMET
EARTH
LIGHT
ORBIT
SPACE

CLOWN MIX-UP

These clowns are all mixed up. Match the correct parts to help the clowns pull themselves together. Hint: Kiki's shoes are in box P.

Tiny

Flip

C.

D.

G.

H.

K.

L.

O.

P.

WHAT AM I?

Can you guess the answer before you reach the last clue?

1. You have seen someone use me. It might even be you.

2. I often have a picture of someone famous on my outside.

3. My inside changes daily.

4. Sometimes you like what's inside me. Other times you might not.

5. I have a handle so you can carry me to school.

6. When kids forget me, I end up in the Lost and Found.

7. I can be made of metal or plastic or both.

8. I see a lot of others like myself in the lunchroom.

9. Some people use a bag instead of me.

Answer on page 50.

ANSWERS

COVER

WHO'S LOOKING AT YOU? (page 3)

1. parrot
2. owl
3. chimpanzee
4. tiger
5. fish
6. frog

THE HAIRCUT (page 6)

2.	5.
3.	1.
6.	4.

NUTS AND BOLTS (page 7)

1. hammer
2. drill
3. tape measure
4. bolt
5. shovel
6. screwdriver
7. monkey wrench

COOL IT (page 8)

These things belong in the refrigerator:
turkey, lettuce, hot dogs, eggs, cheese, milk, butter

MISSING LETTER (page 10)

The missing letter is "W," unless you look at the puzzle upside down. Then the missing letter is "M."

SCRAMBLED BIRDS (page 11)

a. dove
b. crow
c. hawk
d. swan
e. robin
f. stork
g. goose
h. pigeon
i. parrot
j. sparrow
k. penguin
l. flamingo
m. cardinal

Because they don't know the words.

DOWN-ON-THE-FARM CROSSWORD (page 12)

CLIMB TIME (page 14)

DOT'S DEPARTMENT STORE (page 15)

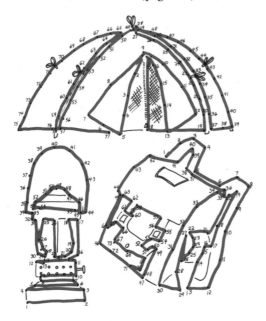

EYE FOOLERS (page 16)

These pictures are called optical illusions, because they trick your eyes. The objects seem to be different sizes, but with a ruler you can prove these answers are true.

1. All three people are the same height.
2. Both circles are the same size.
3. All three circles are the same size.
4. The thin lines are parallel.
5. All four lines are the same length.
6. The objects are all the same length.
7. The two thin lines are the same length.
8. The moon is the same size in both pictures.

WOOD SEARCH (page 19)

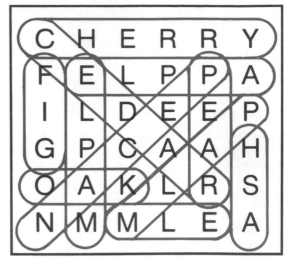

DIGBY'S DINNER (page 20)

Digby's dinner bone is buried under the big rock in the lefthand corner.

TAKE IT TO THE TOP (page 22)

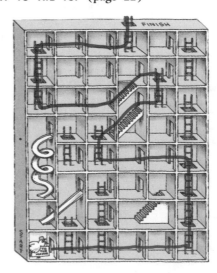

WHAT ON EARTH? (page 23)
When you are Chile (chilly).

PIECE OF CAKE (page 24)

DOZENS OF Ds (page 26)

daffodils
daisies
dancer
dandelions
deer
desk
dial
dirt
dish
diver
diving tank
doctor
dog—a dachshund
dog food

doghouse
doll
dolphin
dome
donkey
door
doorknob
dots
doughnut
dragon
dragonfly
drawer
dress
drops
drumstick
duck

WHAT GOES WITH WHAT? (page 28)

1. C
2. A
3. B
4. J
5. G

6. F
7. I
8. H
9. E
10. D

TUMBLEWORDS (page 32)

baseball
football
golf

hockey
tennis
volleyball

INSTANT PICTURE (page 33)

STOP, LOOK, AND LIST (page 34)

American Cities	Flowers
Tacoma	Tulip
Chicago	Carnation
Phoenix	Poppy
Boston	Buttercup
Orlando	Orchid

Breakfast Foods
Toast
Cereal
Pancakes
Bacon
Orange Juice

SEASHORE MEMORIES (page 36)

1. The boys made a castle out of sand.
2. There was one dolphin.
3. The girl was eating an apple.
4. The inner tube was yellow.
5. There were two sailboats.
6. Yes, one woman had a radio.
7. The dog was sleeping.
8. One person wore sunglasses.

WHICH CLASSROOM? (page 36)

Nathan's teacher is Mr. Franklin.
Sarah's teacher is Ms. Heinz.
Ben's teacher is Ms. DeCaro.

TEST PATTERNS (page 37)

Screen 3 shows the most shapes: 20 squares.

DINNER IS SERVED (page 38)

1. Humpty Dumpty will sit on the wall.
2. Miss Muffet will sit on the tuffet.
3. Miss Muffet's guest, the spider, will sit beside her in the web.
4. Papa Bear, Mama Bear, and Baby Bear will sit in the matching large, medium, and small chairs.
5. The caterpillar will sit on the mushroom.
6. Curlylocks will sit on the cushion.
7. Little Jack Horner will sit in the corner.
8. Old King Cole will sit on the throne.

OLD MEXICO (page 39)

SPEAKING IN COLOR (page 40)

1. B. If you have a green thumb, you can grow plants very well.
2. C. If your sister is seeing red, she is angry.
3. C. If a hero has a yellow streak, he is not very brave.
4. C. If your neighbor is feeling blue, she is sad.
5. C. If you are wearing rose-colored glasses, you have a positive attitude.
6. B. If your friend is green with envy, he is jealous.
7. B. If you are in the pink, you are very healthy.
8. B. If today is a red-letter day, it is very important.

CRISSCROSS COUNTDOWN (page 42)

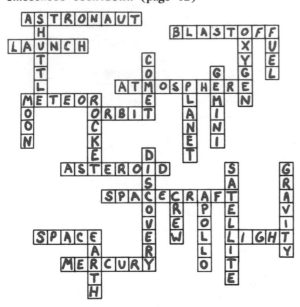

CLOWN MIX-UP (page 44)

Kiki = A, G, J, P
Bobo = B, H, I, O
Tiny = C, E, K, N
Flip = D, F, L, M

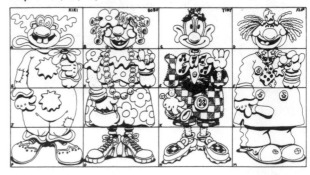

WHAT AM I? (page 46)

A lunchbox